RANGER in TIME

Hurricane Katrina Rescue

THE RANGER IN TIME SERIES

Hurricane Katrina Rescue

KATE MESSNER

illustrated by
KELLEY McMORRIS

Scholastic Inc.

Library of Congress Cataloging-in-Publication Data
Names: Messner, Kate, author. | McMorris, Kelley, illustrator. | Messner, Kate. Ranger in time.
Title: Hurricane Katrina rescue / Kate Messner ; illustrated by Kelley McMorris.
Description: New York : Scholastic Inc., [2018] | Series: Ranger in time | Summary: When the mysterious first aid kit takes golden retriever Ranger to New Orleans shortly before Hurricane Katrina hits, he finds himself helping Clare Porter and her grandmother, who are waiting for Clare's father at their home in the Lower Ninth Ward — and when the levees break and Clare is separated from Nana, Ranger must somehow get her to the relative safety of the Superdome, and reunite her with her family.
Identifiers: LCCN 2017047764
Subjects: LCSH: Hurricane Katrina, 2005 — Juvenile fiction. | Golden retriever — Juvenile fiction. | Time travel — Juvenile fiction. | Families — Louisiana — New Orleans — Juvenile fiction. | Adventure stories. | Ninth Ward (New Orleans, La.) — Juvenile fiction. | New Orleans (La.) — History — 21st century — Juvenile fiction. | CYAC: Hurricane Katrina, 2005 — Fiction. | Golden retriever — Fiction. | Dogs — Fiction. | Time travel — Fiction. | Family life — Louisiana — New Orleans — Fiction. | Adventure and adventurers — Fiction. | New Orleans (La.) — Fiction. | GSAFD: Adventure fiction. | LCGFT: Action and adventure fiction.
Classification: LCC PZ10.3.M5635 Hu 2018 | DDC 813.6 [Fic] — dc23
LC record available at https://lccn.loc.gov/2017047764

ISBN 978-1-338-13395-0

10 9 8 7 6 5 4 3   18 19 20 21 22

Printed in the United States of America   40
First printing 2018

Book design by Ellen Duda and Maeve Norton

*For all the residents of the Lower Ninth Ward,
yesterday and today*

Chapter 1

TIME TO GO

When Clare Porter's dad dropped her off to volunteer at the SPCA on Saturday morning, the neighborhood hummed with activity. Traffic helicopters buzzed overhead. Neighbors hammered plywood over windows, getting ready for the storm. Two big trucks were parked outside the animal shelter.

"What's going on?" Clare asked James, one of the older volunteers.

"We're moving the animals to Houston," James told her. "Katrina is a Category Three hurricane now. Procedure says we have to evacuate the shelter. I'm working on ID collars. We also need to take photos of all the dogs and cats before they're loaded onto the truck." He handed Clare a camera, and she set to work.

"Smile, Bugsy!" she told a grumpy bulldog mix. She'd met him on her first day volunteering at the shelter last fall, right after she'd turned eleven.

"Your family leaving?" James asked Clare as he fastened a collar on a squirmy orange cat.

"Mom and my little brothers have been visiting Aunt Celeste in Houston. They're going to stay a few extra days," Clare said. "Daddy and I are staying here with my grandmother to ride out the storm unless it gets real bad."

James raised his eyebrows. "Already starting to look like a big one."

"We'll be careful." Clare looked at the pale, quiet sky. It was hard to imagine a monster hurricane just two days away. Aside from getting their houses ready, most of her neighbors in the Lower Ninth Ward of New Orleans were going about their business. Dad had taken Nana to basketball practice right after he'd dropped Clare off to work at the shelter. Nana used to be one of the star players on the Silver Slammers, a basketball team for women sixty years and older. But Nana was eighty now, and last year, she started forgetting things. She couldn't remember the rules. She couldn't really play in games anymore, but she still went to practice to shoot baskets. Practice had gone on today, just like always.

But by the time Clare's father picked her up at the shelter, more and more neighbors were packing their cars.

"We've got time," Dad said. He scooped some of Nana's red beans and rice into a bowl for dinner and limped over to the table. His knee still bothered him from when he got hurt in the army a long time ago.

"I still think the storm will turn," Dad said. "We'll wait and see."

Later, after she was in bed, Clare heard him on the phone with her mother. "I know. But evacuation would be mandatory if they thought the storm was going to hit that hard . . . Okay . . . Love you, too."

On Sunday morning, Clare woke to the sound of the news on TV.

"Devastating damage is expected, rivaling the intensity of Hurricane Camille of 1969 . . ."

Clare shivered. Dad had told her stories about Camille. Back then the flooding was so bad that he and Grandpa had to break out of their attic with an axe and wait on the roof to be rescued.

"Clare?" Dad called. Clare found him in the kitchen at the front of their long, skinny house, filling a cooler. "The mayor just ordered a mandatory evacuation. We're leaving. Pack clothes for a week," he told her.

"A week?!"

"Just in case," Dad said. "Storm's getting stronger. I'm going to put gas in the car. Mrs. Jackson next door is coming with us, too."

"Mrs. Jackson? How come?" Clare asked.

"She doesn't have family here," Dad said. "So we need to look out for her. No one gets left behind on my watch."

Clare nodded. She hadn't been born yet when her father served in the army during Operation Desert Storm, but she knew the story of how he got hurt. He'd run out from behind a jeep to rescue another soldier who had fallen during a firefight. Dad said he had to go, even though it was dangerous. You never leave a fallen soldier. It was an army promise. The mission wasn't over until everyone made it out.

"We'll leave as soon as I get back," Dad said. "Keep an eye on Nana while I'm gone."

"Okay." Clare headed down the hallway. "Are you getting clothes together, Nana?" she called into her grandmother's bedroom.

"I'm staying right here," Nana said. "I have practice tonight." She held up her Silver Slammers warm-up jacket.

Clare sighed. "There won't be practice with the storm, Nana. Everyone's leaving. Pack your clothes, okay?"

Clare went to her bedroom and threw shorts and T-shirts into a backpack. She was in the middle of reading *Bud, Not Buddy* again, so she packed that, too. Then she took it back out to read as she waited for Dad. She liked all of Bud's funny rules for getting by in the world.

After a while, the wind rattled her window, and Clare looked up. It had already been half an hour. Just how far did Dad have to go for gas? Clare hoped he'd find an open station soon so they could head out.

The sky grew darker and darker. Clare turned on a light. The wind slammed a door shut somewhere. Clare looked at the clock. It was already noon. She texted her father.

When will you be home?

He didn't reply. So Clare turned on the radio.

"At least one-half of well-constructed homes will have roof and wall failure," an announcer said. "Water shortages will make human suffering incredible by modern standards. Once tropical storm and hurricane force winds onset, do not venture outside."

Clare closed her book. She rushed to the living room. The door was partway open, thumping back and forth on its hinges. Clare looked out. There was no sign of Dad. And the rain had already started. She closed the door tight.

He'll be here soon, Clare thought. *We just need to get everything ready so we can leave right away when he comes back.*

"Nana!" she called. "Are you all packed?"

Her grandmother didn't respond. "Nana!" Clare called again. She ran to Nana's bedroom. It was empty.

Panic rose in Clare's chest. How many pages ago had she heard the door slam? How long had it been since Nana wandered off?

Clare raced to the front door and yanked it open. Her grandmother's warm-up jacket was on the porch swing. Clare grabbed it and held it to her chest. "Nana!" she shouted into the rain.

But only the wind answered back.

Chapter 2

RUMBLING SKY

"Whoops!" Sadie looked down at the last bite of hot dog that had slipped off her plate onto the grass.

"Hey, Ranger!" Luke said. "Looks like you get an extra treat!"

Ranger hurried over and gobbled it up. He loved hot dogs. And he loved it when Luke and Sadie's family had cookouts with their friends, the Tarrars. Someone was always dropping something.

Ranger sniffed around the picnic table

until a flash of brown near the garden caught his eye.

Squirrel!

Ranger ran after the squirrel, barking. He chased it through Mom's herbs and past the sunflowers. He chased it up and down the porch steps and around the picnic table. Finally, the squirrel raced up a tall tree. It sat on a branch, chattering down at Ranger.

Ranger barked a couple of times. Then he went back to sniff for more hot-dog pieces. Ranger had never caught a squirrel, but he loved chasing them. Squirrels were the reason he wasn't an official search-and-rescue dog.

Ranger had done weeks of search-and-rescue training with Luke and Dad. He'd learned to follow a scent trail to find a missing person. He'd practiced finding Luke in all kinds of odd places. He'd found Luke hiding

in barrels and behind tree stumps. He'd even found him once when he was buried in the snow! Ranger was good at finding people.

But in order to be a search-and-rescue dog, you had to pass a special test. You had to ignore everything around you except the command you'd been given. You had to ignore dog treats and toys and juicy pieces of hot dogs. You even had to ignore squirrels.

On the day of Ranger's test, a squirrel had run by, swishing its fluffy tail. Ranger had chased it. He wouldn't have done that if a real person needed help. But he knew Luke was just pretending to be lost, like always. So Ranger didn't pass his test.

But he was still good at finding things. Like hot dogs!

Ranger sniffed around under the picnic table until he found another piece Sadie had dropped.

Then the sky let out a rumble.

"Uh-oh," said Luke's mom. "We'd better move this party inside for dessert. Dad has peanut butter cookies in the oven."

Everyone started picking up plates and food, but Ranger went straight to the door. He pawed at it and whined.

Ranger did not like storms. Thunder made the hair on his neck feel all nervous and prickly.

"You want to go inside, Ranger?" Luke said, and opened the door. "Go on. We'll be right there."

Ranger went to his dog bed in the mud-room so he could curl up in his blanket and wait for the storm to go away. Another rumble of thunder shook the sky, and Ranger whimpered. Then he heard a quieter humming sound.

Ranger knew that sound. It was coming

from a mysterious first aid kit he'd dug up from the garden one day. The old metal box made a humming sound whenever someone far away needed his help. Once, the box took Ranger to a loud, scary beach where two young men were in danger. Another time, it had taken him to a land of ash and smoke, where he'd met a girl named Helga.

Ranger pawed at his blanket until he uncovered the old first aid kit. Beside it were some of Ranger's treasures — bits of paper and metal and two feathers — things he'd brought back from his adventures the other times the old metal box had hummed. The box had taken Ranger to busy cities, frozen oceans, and quiet prairies — always because someone needed his help.

Now it was humming again.

Ranger pawed the leather strap over his head. The humming got louder and louder.

Light began to spill from the cracks in the old metal box. It grew brighter and brighter, until Ranger had to close his eyes. The first aid kit grew warm at his neck, and he felt as if he were being squeezed through a hole in the sky.

Finally, the humming stopped and the box cooled.

When Ranger opened his eyes, rain blew into them.

But this wasn't the crisp, cool rain of home. The air here was hot, muggy, and thick. The wind rattled a street sign. Then a girl called out.

"Nana! Nana, where are you?"

Chapter 3

STORM WARNING

Ranger ran up to the girl, but she barely looked at him. "Nana!" she called. She ran to the house next door and pounded the door. Ranger followed her.

A man on a bicycle called from the street. "They left town yesterday!"

"Oh!" Clare whirled around so fast she almost tripped over Ranger.

"Have you seen my grandmother?" she asked the man, and held out a warm-up jacket. "Nana left this. She wanders sometimes. We're supposed to be leaving . . ."

"Haven't seen her, but I'll take a lap and let you know if I do," the man said.

"Thank you. I have to find her!" Clare said as he rode off.

Find!

Ranger barked. That was the command Luke and Dad used in training sessions. Luke would run and hide in the woods. Dad would say, "Are you ready, boy? Go find Luke! Find him!" Ranger would take off, sniffing the air and the ground until he tracked Luke's scent to wherever he was hiding.

Ranger sniffed the jacket in the girl's hands. It held another person's scent, too. Maybe the Nana person!

Ranger barked again. "That's my grandmother's jacket," the girl said. "Do you smell her? I have to find her."

Find! Ranger walked down the sidewalk. The air smelled of rain and dirt and sawdust.

Ranger could smell the girl and the man on the bike. But no Nana smell. Not yet.

Ranger circled, and the girl followed him back toward her house.

There!

The Nana smell!

Ranger followed the scent trail down the block, into a grassy yard. The Nana scent was getting stronger.

"Where are you going?" Clare stepped around some tomato plants in a garden. "This is where Nana's friend Ruth lives, but she's gone."

Ranger ran up the porch steps and pawed at an old screen door. On the other side, Nana sat quietly on an old sofa.

"Nana!" Clare opened the door and rushed in. "What are you doing?"

Nana looked confused. "I'm waiting for Ruth. We have basketball."

"There's no practice because of the storm," Clare said. "Ruth is on her way to Baton Rouge. We're going to Houston as soon as Daddy gets home. Come on."

Clare walked her grandmother home. When she got to the door, she looked down at Ranger. "Whose dog are you?" She lifted the first aid kit from around his neck. "Are you with the hurricane rescue people?"

Clare looked up and down the empty street. "You can't stay out in the storm." She held open the door. "Come on."

Ranger followed her inside. The house was cozy, but the wind had a dangerous sound. Ranger settled on a throw rug while Clare checked her phone. There was still no word from her father. She tried calling him but got his voice mail.

"Dad, it's me," Clare said. "Is everything all right? Because it's been a really long time and

I hope you're on your way home. Call me, please. I'll keep getting things ready."

Ranger followed Clare into the kitchen. He sat by the stove while she finished filling the cooler.

At five o'clock, it started to rain harder. Clare called her father again. This time, the call didn't even go through. She heated up leftovers for supper. She turned on the radio, but reports of traffic jams and gas shortages made her stomach hurt.

By nine o'clock, the rain was coming sideways in sheets, battering the windows. Clare's stomach felt all tied up in knots. Where was her father? She peered out the front window. There wasn't a single car on the street. Where was he? What if he'd run out of gas? What if he was stranded somewhere?

Nana was in her bedroom listening to music. Clare didn't want to worry or confuse

her any more. She'd simply tell Nana the plan had changed. They would stay in New Orleans after all. Nana would be happy about that.

Clare made a mental list of all the things her parents did to prepare for hurricanes. She gathered flashlights and batteries. She found the family's folder of important papers and put it in a big plastic bin with their photo albums.

Ranger wasn't sure how to help, so he followed Clare around. She seemed happy to have company as she lugged the bin up to the attic. She brought Ranger's first aid kit, too. It might come in handy in a storm.

Finally, Clare collapsed on the couch. Wind shook the windows, and rain pounded the roof. It was almost eleven o'clock. Nana had gone to sleep a long time ago, but Clare was afraid to go to bed. What if Nana wandered out into the storm?

Clare curled up on the sofa. Ranger jumped up next to her. She wrapped an arm around him and closed her eyes. But she couldn't stop thinking about her father, out there somewhere in the rain and wind.

She kept imagining him in that other storm a long time ago, trapped in the attic as water rose around him.

The axe! Clare sat up. She reached over to turn on the light, but the power was out. She grabbed a flashlight and ran to the back porch. Her sneakers crunched on broken glass as soon as she stepped out of the kitchen. The storm had blown out two windows. Rain whipped in from the darkness, so hard it felt like sand against her face.

She grabbed the axe from the corner by her father's toolbox, ran inside, and bounded up the stairs to the attic. She leaned the axe against the plastic bin. Then she went back down and stretched out on the couch with Ranger beside her.

All night long, Clare tossed and turned, listening to the pounding rain. Every time she started to doze off, wind shook the house and she jerked awake. What could have happened to her father? Wherever he was, Clare hoped he'd found shelter. *Let him be safe*, she prayed. *And please let him come home soon.*

Finally, the sky outside grew light again. It was still raining, but the wind had quieted. Clare patted Ranger's head. "Maybe the worst is over," she said.

There was an inch or so of water in the living room. They'd have to clean up when Dad got home. Maybe he was on his way now that the storm had let up.

Clare sloshed to the front door, unbolted

the lock, opened it, and peeked outside. It looked as if a giant had stomped through her neighborhood. The storm had snapped trees and scattered roofing everywhere. But the Lower Ninth Ward had survived, like always.

Ranger stood beside her, sniffing the wet morning air. It smelled of rain and gasoline and mud.

Clare was about to close the door when she heard a loud boom.

Then there was a roaring, rushing sound. Soon, waves of water were surging down the street. It could only mean one thing.

"Get upstairs, Nana!" Clare shouted. "The levee broke!"

Chapter 4

RISING WATERS

Clare slammed the door shut. Nana hurried into the living room in her slippers.

"The levee's breached. Look!" Clare pointed to the front door. A waterfall poured in through the mail slot. "We need to get to the attic!" The water in the living room was up to Clare's ankles. How high would it rise? And how fast?

Clare ran through the house to her bedroom. She grabbed her backpack full of clothes and her book. What if the whole house flooded? Clare looked at the clarinet and music books under her desk, her bulletin board covered with report cards and SPCA volunteer certificates. Should she try to fill another bag?

Ranger stood in the doorway. The whole house was vibrating in the rushing flood. He could feel it under his paws. He barked, and Clare turned to look.

The house groaned, and something thumped against the siding. The time for packing was over.

"Nana, come on!" Clare led her grandmother up to the attic. She dropped her backpack on the wooden floor and helped Nana settle on one of the sleeping bags they used when they camped near Lake Pontchartrain in the summer.

"You okay for now?" Clare asked.

Nana nodded and pulled her knitting from her bag. "Don't you worry, baby," Nana said. "Your daddy'll be back soon."

"Wait here," Clare said. "I'm going to get us some water and food."

Clare turned back to the stairs. Ranger stayed so close she almost tripped over him. She'd taken only two steps down when her breath caught in her throat. The water was covering the bottom stairs. How could it be rising so fast?

"Lord," Clare whispered. But they couldn't stay in that stifling attic without drinking water. Clare stepped into the flood and pushed forward. It was already up to her knees.

Ranger splashed after her through the living room. The little wooden end table was flipped, legs in the air, floating toward the doorway. Clare pushed it out of the way and struggled into the kitchen. The refrigerator had toppled over onto its door, so she couldn't get to anything inside. Clare grabbed two bottles of water from a high shelf. She bent over

and felt around under the filthy water. Where was the cooler they had packed?

Ranger tried to hold his chin up, but soon, waves of water swept his paws out from under him, and he was paddling.

Ranger barked. It wasn't safe here! They had to get back where it was dry.

"Go on!" Clare came up sputtering, her shirt dripping with muck. "Go up with Nana! I'm coming!"

Clare snatched a loaf of bread and a box of garbage bags that were floating by. They needed more food. She needed more time! How could it be so deep already?

Ranger pawed at Clare, struggling to stay above the awful, sharp-smelling water. It was nothing like the lake where he swam with Luke and Sadie at home. This water smelled of waste and gasoline. It wasn't safe. Clare had to get out of it.

She understood that, too. "Come on, dog," she said, and fought her way through the water, nudging him along with her leg.

The current threatened to push her over. How could there be a current in her house?

Clare reached for the couch to steady herself, but that was floating, too. There was nothing to grab.

Ranger felt her hand on his back and struggled to keep himself afloat. He paddled through the living room, until his paws finally touched the stairs.

Clare climbed five steps and sank down beside him, her arms full of soggy bread and water bottles. She stared into the living room, at all of her family's things — tables and books and board games — all floating in the stinking water.

There was barely time to catch her breath. In seconds, the flood was licking at her sneakers.

Clare slogged up the stairs. She climbed into the attic and closed the door.

"You get some water?" Nana asked from the corner by the vent. Wet curls stuck to her forehead. She dabbed at her face with the purple bandanna she wore at basketball practice.

"Here." Clare handed her one of the bottles. Nana opened it and took a long drink.

Clare knelt by the vent and tried to see outside. The rain had stopped, but water gushed down the street. It felt as if their house had landed in the middle of the Mississippi.

"Help should come soon, Nana," Clare said, but she had no idea if that was true.

"Pray they make it fast," Nana said. She took a shaky breath, leaned back against the wall, and closed her eyes.

Clare dragged another sleeping bag from the camping things and spread it out.

Ranger looked up at her.

"Go on, dog," Clare said. "There's room for you." So he curled up on the slippery red nylon. Clare pulled *Bud, Not Buddy* from her bag and sat beside him, leaning against the wall.

She tried to get lost in the story with Bud and his rules, but her eyes strayed to the attic door.

Where was the water now?

Could it rise high enough to fill the attic?

If it did, where would they go? How would they even get out?

Clare's eyes fell on the axe in the corner. She hoped she wouldn't need it. And she prayed she'd be strong enough to use it if she did.

Chapter 5

THE AXE IN THE ATTIC

Clare forced herself to read, but every few minutes, something thumped against the house and shook the attic floor. Trees? Cars? Other houses?

Ranger sat quietly at Clare's side. His skin prickled under his fur. The attic air was hot and wet and stale, filled with the smell of old things and dampness. Other smells drifted in through the vent. Gasoline and chemicals. Dirty water and torn-up earth. The roar of the water seemed like it would never end.

But after a while, it changed. Along with the

rush of the flood out in the street, there was a closer splashing. A gurgle at the attic door.

Ranger ran to the door and barked. Water was seeping in through the cracks around the frame, already spreading over the attic's worn wooden floor.

Clare looked up from her book and gasped. How long had it been? Ten minutes? Fifteen? How could the water have climbed the stairs already?

"Nana, get up!" Clare shook her grandmother's arm and then pointed to the attic door. Water poured in underneath. It was seeping up through the floorboards, too. Soon, the sleeping bags would be soaked.

"Here . . ." Clare dragged the plastic bin to the corner. "Sit here so you stay dry." She was thankful when Nana didn't argue.

Then Clare picked up the axe. It was heavier than she remembered, even from yesterday.

She looked up at the beams and boards that crisscrossed the ceiling. They seemed impossibly sturdy.

But the water was already over her sneakers. If it kept rising, they'd need a way to get out.

"Watch out, dog." Clare took a deep breath. She lifted the axe and let the head fall behind her. She chose a spot on the ceiling and swung the axe upward as hard as she could.

It made a tiny chip in the wood.

She swung again. And again. The muscles in her arms burned.

"We should go downstairs," Nana said, standing up.

"Nana, no." Clare wanted to cry. "We can't go down. We can't open the door. Just . . . please . . . stay there."

Ranger understood the command *stay*. He understood that Clare needed his help.

He couldn't whack at the ceiling with her, but he could keep Nana settled.

Ranger sloshed through the water to Nana's side. She looked down and gave him a pat on the head. "Aren't you a good dog. You need a bath, though."

Ranger nuzzled Nana's hand. He nudged her back to the plastic bin. She sat down and stroked his wet fur.

Every time Clare swung the axe, dust rained down on her. The water was up to her shins, and she hadn't even made the tiniest hole in the ceiling. It was impossible to get any momentum when she had to swing upward. She was never going to break through.

Clare swallowed hard, but the lump growing in her throat only got bigger. There was no time to cry. She had to get Nana out of here before they both drowned.

Clare's eyes burned with the sharp smell of

the filthy, rising water. She lifted the axe and took another whack at the ceiling. The axe stuck in the wood. She had to pull and twist to get it free. When the board finally let the axe go, there was barely a dent in it.

Clare's arms trembled, but she lifted the axe again. Maybe lots of smaller swings would be faster. She hacked away at the board above her. Tiny wood chips flew everywhere. But there was no rush of fresh air from the outside. No sliver of sky to give her hope. No escape from the rising water.

Clare struggled to catch her breath, but the hot, stinking air in the attic made her cough. Even if the water stopped rising, she knew they couldn't survive here for long.

Chapter 6

No Room on the Boat

When Clare couldn't hold the axe any longer, she dropped it and collapsed against the wall. Tears streamed down her cheeks, and she let out a sob.

Ranger sloshed over to Clare and nuzzled her hand. That made her cry harder. Even the dog was depending on her, but her arms were too tired. The flood was going to swallow them up. How long would it be? An hour? Two?

Clare looked down at the water around her knees. Had it finally stopped rising?

She waded through the muck to Nana, who was still perched on the bin, leaning into the corner. Somehow, she'd managed to doze off, even with Clare chopping at the ceiling. Clare found their old kitchen table in another corner. She dragged it over and spread a damp sleeping bag on top.

"Nana . . ." Clare shook her grandmother awake and helped her onto the table. Then she pulled a trunk over by the bin, sat down on it, and patted the bin. "Come on up, dog. Get out of the water."

Ranger jumped up and sat down. He was soaked. But at least he was with Clare.

Clare pulled her legs in tight so she'd fit on the trunk. She read her book, stopping every few chapters to nudge Nana awake and get her to have a drink of water. The attic grew warmer and warmer. Clare turned pages and worried and waited for help. But no one came. She didn't know what time it was, but the light coming through the vent was getting dim. And she was exhausted.

Why hadn't her father come back? Where was he? Clare reached for her phone, but it didn't turn on. Somehow, in all her preparations, she'd forgotten to charge it.

Clare's eyes burned with tears. She blinked them away and took a few deep breaths. She needed to stay calm. She needed to stay strong. And right now, she needed sleep. In the morning, she'd pick up the axe and try again . . .

"Anybody there?" a deep voice called. Clare was sleeping, but Ranger heard it. He jumped from the trunk, splashed through the water to the vent, and barked.

Clare sat up. The sky was just getting light. "What is it, dog?"

"Anybody there?" the voice called again.

Clare jumped up, ran to the vent, and shouted, "We're here! Help! Please! We're here!"

"Clare?" the man called.

"Yes!" It was her dad's friend Mr. Robinson. "I'm trapped here with Nana!" Clare shouted out the vent. "I've been trying to break out with an axe but it's not working."

"Hold on!" he called. "I'm coming!"

Something clunked against the house. Clare heard footsteps on the roof. Then a voice from above said, "I have an axe. Stay clear and I'll get you out of there!"

A few seconds later, there was a loud *thwack!* Sawdust drifted down from the ceiling.

Nana startled awake. "What's happening?"

"It's all right, Nana," Clare said, and held her grandmother's hand. "Mr. Robinson is here. He's cutting a hole in the roof to get us out."

Thwack! Crack! Thunk!

Finally, a board broke. Light streamed into the attic from above.

Thwack! Crack!

Crash!

"Good Lord!" Mr. Robinson said, leaning in through the opening he'd made. "I thought y'all had decided to leave, but then I saw old Mrs. Jackson on her roof."

"Oh no!" Clare felt awful. She should have checked on Mrs. Jackson somehow. "Is she all right?"

Mr. Robinson nodded. "I've got her in my boat. But where's your dad?"

"He went to find gas for the car. He hasn't come back," Clare said. A hot lump rose in her throat.

"No gas for miles," Mr. Robinson said. "My guess is he got stuck out of town. He'll find his way back, don't you worry."

Clare nodded.

Mr. Robinson pointed to the trunk. "Shove that over here so you can climb out."

Clare pulled the old trunk by its scratchy rope handle until it was below the jagged hole in the attic roof. She helped Nana climb up first.

"Don't worry. I've got you," Mr. Robinson said, and lifted Nana onto the roof.

Clare thumped the wooden trunk. "Go on, dog! Go up and wait with Nana."

Ranger jumped onto the trunk and leaped from there onto the roof.

The shingles were wet and slimy-scratchy under his paws. Ranger spread his toes so he wouldn't slip. He padded over to Nana and sat down beside her while Clare handed supplies up to Mr. Robinson.

First, she passed him Nana's bag and a life jacket she'd found with their camping things.

She loaded her backpack, Ranger's first aid kit, the bread, and her last bottle of water into a garbage bag and sent that up. Then she hoisted herself onto the roof.

Mr. Robinson looked down at Clare, his forehead creased with worry. "Thing is . . . I can't take you both," he said. "I've already got three others." He nodded down at the boat where his wife and mother-in-law were waiting with Mrs. Jackson from next door.

Clare knew what needed to happen. "Take Nana," she said. "Please. She's not doing well with the heat."

Mr. Robinson hesitated, but Clare helped Nana into the life jacket.

"All right then," he said. "Once we make it to the bridge, I'll walk her to the Superdome. It's set up as a shelter with doctors and such. She'll be in good hands. And it won't be long before the Coast Guard brings you there, too.

Here . . ." He picked up Nana's purple bandanna from where she'd dropped it on the roof and handed it to Clare. "Wave this when you see the boats coming. Make sure they see you." Then Mr. Robinson lowered himself off the roof.

Clare tucked the bandanna in a pocket and turned to Nana. She put her hands on her grandmother's shoulders and looked in her eyes. "Nana, Mr. Robinson's taking you to a shelter." Clare swallowed hard. "I'll meet you there soon."

"Hope it's cooler there," Nana said, and Clare knew she wasn't thinking clearly. If she had been, she'd never agree to leave Clare alone. But she let Clare help her down into the Robinsons' boat.

"Thank you!" Clare called to Mr. Robinson. Her eyes burned with tears as she watched them go.

Ranger crept to the edge of the roof. He pawed at Clare until she scrambled up higher, away from the deep, dark water. Then he sat beside her and leaned his body into hers.

"It's okay, dog," Clare said. She scratched him behind his ear. "Help will come soon."

She hoped what she said would be true.

Chapter 7

LEAP OF FAITH

When Clare couldn't see Mr. Robinson's boat anymore, she fished around in her garbage bag. She pulled out the bottle of water and took a long drink. The water was warm, but it still tasted good. Clare took a deep breath and tried to quiet her racing thoughts.

Everything would be all right. It had to be. Mr. Robinson would be back soon. And her father, too. He was probably on his way.

Clare set the water bottle down and reached for her book. When she turned, the bottle slid down the sloped roof.

"Oh no!" Clare jumped up — too fast! Her feet flew out from under her, and she landed flat on her back. She kicked and clawed at the slick roof, trying to catch herself as she skidded toward the filthy water. The shingles scraped her hands and elbows raw.

Finally, her foot caught something and she stopped sliding.

Clare lay pressed against the wet roof, praying the flimsy aluminum gutter wouldn't break and dump her into the dark water below.

Ranger barked. He couldn't drag Clare up from the edge of the roof. But maybe he could help her find a way to safety. Carefully, he started down the roof toward her. He tested each step with his paw to see how slick the shingles were. Parts of the roof were less slippery, and when he finally reached Clare, he nudged her in that direction.

Slowly and carefully, Clare wiggled sideways

until she found a less slippery spot. She started inching her way up the roof. But then she spotted her water bottle in the gutter. Did she dare reach for it and risk slipping again? Clare was afraid to move, but she knew she couldn't give up her only water. She eased her way down, inch by inch, and grabbed the bottle. Then she crawled back up to her bag and collapsed beside it.

"You all right there?" a voice called. A skinny man was drifting by on an old door he'd made into a raft. He leaned forward, paddling with a folded-up piece of cardboard.

"I'm okay!" Clare called, suddenly aware of how alone she was. This man wasn't anyone she recognized from the neighborhood. "Help is coming!" The man nodded and continued down the flooded street.

Clare read her book and slapped at mosquitoes that seemed to multiply by the hour. She kept Nana's purple bandanna by her side, ready to wave as soon as she spotted a boat. But the Coast Guard never came.

The sun sank lower in the sky. When Clare couldn't stand the swarming insects anymore, she lowered herself into the attic. Ranger jumped down onto the trunk, too. They both sloshed through the flood and curled up on Nana's sleeping-bag table. There wasn't much room, and it was way too hot, but Clare was thankful for the shaggy dog. She was too scared to spend the night alone and barely slept anyway.

When light spilled through the hole in the ceiling again, Clare climbed back onto the roof, and Ranger jumped up after her.

There were no boats. No people. She wished Mr. Robinson would come back. Or, better yet, her dad. She'd even take the stranger from yesterday now, with his front-door raft.

"Too bad we don't have a door, dog," Clare said. The man had been paddling on one side to turn, just the way her father did when he was steering their pirogue, the old flat-bottomed boat they used to go crabbing on Lake Pontchartrain.

"The pirogue!" Clare said. She looked at Ranger. "We don't need a door, dog! We have a boat! At least, I hope we do . . ."

Her father kept the pirogue tied to the shed behind the house. Clare stood up to look into the backyard. Yes!

In the attic, she found the wooden paddle her father used with the boat and brought it up to the roof. The pirogue was tugging at its rope in the flood, like an animal that wanted to get away. Clare looked out over the water that separated her from the boat. It was at least twenty feet. Not too far to swim. But this wasn't ordinary water.

Clare wished she had something to keep her afloat. She crawled around the edge of the house to see if there might be a board or something in the water. All kinds of things floated by. Coolers and roof shingles and base-ball caps. Plastic bags and kickballs and a lonely rubber boot. Then Clare saw a flash of orange.

"A life jacket!" Clare didn't let herself think about whose it was or what might have hap-pened to them. She crawled to the edge of the roof and waited for it to come closer. It was dirty and faded, tangled in thick, dark ropes. But it would help her get to the boat. That was enough.

Clare held the paddle out and poked at the life jacket, trying to pull it closer.

Ranger crouched low beside her, sniffing the air. The water still smelled of chemicals and torn-up earth. But as Clare pulled the old life jacket closer, he smelled something else. Something dangerous!

Ranger barked and pawed at Clare.

"Stop it, dog!" she said.

But Ranger wouldn't stop barking.

Clare squinted at the old life jacket. The ropes around it were moving!

Clare sucked in her breath. "Snakes!" Dark patterned water moccasins writhed around the life jacket's straps. Clare had seen venomous snakes like these near the lake with her father. He'd warned her to stay away.

But Clare wasn't about to give up. She raised the paddle and smacked it down hard on the life jacket. Two thick snakes untangled themselves and wiggled away. They curled around each other and drifted with the current.

Clare took a shaky breath and dragged the life jacket onto the roof. She felt a sharp sting on one hand as she untangled the straps.

"Ah! Fire ants!" she cried. The life jacket was crawling with them. Just like the water moccasins, they must have been flooded out of their homes. They were clinging to whatever they could to survive.

Clare shook out the life jacket until the ants were gone. She put it on and looked across the water at the little pirogue, bobbing beside the shed. If she spent any more time thinking about what might be in that water, she'd never get the boat. Clare turned to Ranger.

"Stay, dog," she said. "Stay."

Then she grabbed the paddle and leaped off the roof into the water.

Chapter 8

INTO THE FLOOD

Clare held her breath and squeezed her eyes closed as she plunged into the stinking water. The tattered life jacket didn't keep her from going under, but once she popped back up, it made swimming easier.

Head for the boat. She had to head for the boat.

Clare paddled and kicked her sneakers. Every time something in the water brushed against her, she imagined the twisting, writhing snakes and tried to swim faster. She could hear the little boat clunking against the wood of the shed. She just had to get there.

Ranger barked. What was Clare doing? Why had she jumped into the awful water? She'd told him to stay, so he did. But he stood on alert at the very edge of the roof, watching.

Clare struggled to hold on to the paddle and keep her face out of the filthy water. Every time she took a breath, she swallowed another mouthful. Finally, she kicked hard, reached out, and felt the rough, splintery wood of the pirogue. She clung to the bow of the little boat, flung the paddle inside, and tried to catch her breath. She'd made it! But the boat was no good to her unless she could get it untied.

Clare shuffled along the edge of the boat until she reached the rope that tied it to the old tree next to the shed. She tried to undo the knot, but the rope was swollen with flood-water. Every time she tugged at it, the knot grew tighter.

Why hadn't she thought to bring the axe from the attic? Even if she swam back to the roof now, she'd never be able to climb back up. What was she going to do?

Something scraped past Clare's leg, way down in the muck, and she shivered. She couldn't stay in the water. So she pulled herself up onto the bow, swung a leg over the side, and flopped into the boat. Something poked her side.

"Ow!" Clare reached down. When she saw what she'd landed on, her heart jumped with hope. It was her father's folded-up fishing knife! Clare flipped open the blade and went at the rope. She sliced and jabbed and hacked. Fiber by fiber, it came apart. Finally, Clare brought the knife down on the last thin strands, and the boat was free!

Clare paddled to the house. When the boat bumped against the edge of the roof, she grabbed the gutter to keep from drifting away. She sat up tall, but her bag was out of reach.

Clare doubted she could make it onto the roof without falling into the water. Even if she did, the boat would drift away before she got back. Why hadn't she thought this through? Her only hope was the dog.

"Hey, dog!" Clare called. "Fetch?"

Ranger looked down at Clare. *Fetch?* That's what Luke and Sadie said when they threw sticks for Ranger. There were lots of sticks in the water. Did Clare want him to fetch one?

"Fetch!" Clare called again. She pointed up onto the roof. "Go get my bag! Fetch! Bring it here!"

She pointed again. Ranger looked behind him and saw the bag. Was that what she wanted? He turned and started toward it.

"That's it! Good dog!" Clare shouted.

Ranger took the knotted handle in his teeth and dragged it to Clare.

"Good job!" Clare stretched her arm up to grab it. "Okay now, ready?" She thumped the boat's little wooden bench with her hand. "Come on! Jump!"

Ranger crept to the very edge of the roof. He didn't like the way the boat kept bobbing up and down. It moved closer and away, closer and away. But if Clare was going in the boat, Ranger had to go, too. So he jumped — and thumped into the bottom of the wooden boat. At least there was a soggy jacket to break his fall.

"Whoops!" Clare said, patting Ranger. She picked up the old orange jacket, held it to her chest, and sighed. "If Dad were here, he'd have us safe and dry by now." She settled herself on the little bench and dipped the paddle into the water.

Ranger curled up at her feet as she paddled through the flooded streets. He was tired, but he didn't close his eyes. Everything felt wrong in this strange, watery place. The city was so quiet. There was a gurgle and splash every time Clare pulled the paddle through the water and, somewhere, the choppy hum of a faraway helicopter. And then another sound.

Ranger perked up his ears. There it was again. A person sound! It was coming from the house they'd just floated past.

Ranger barked. He scrambled to the back of the boat.

"Settle down, dog, or you're going to end up in the water." Clare paddled toward the bridge at the end of the street. But the dog

wouldn't stop barking. Finally, he pawed at her arm, and she turned. "What is it?"

The dog didn't answer. But Clare heard someone else's voice.

"Help! Is anyone there?" a woman called.

And then, a baby's cry.

Chapter 9

THE LITTLEST SURVIVOR

Clare twisted around. The voice had come from behind her. She paddled hard on one side to turn the boat. Then she headed back up the street.

"Where are you?" Clare shouted. "I have a boat and I'm coming!"

"Here!" the voice called. Clare scanned the rooftops, searching for someone who might have escaped from an attic like she and Nana had. She didn't see anyone until the woman shouted again. "Over here!"

Finally, Clare saw a woman waving an old

shirt out an attic window. In her other arm, she cradled a baby who couldn't have been more than a few months old.

"I see you! I'm coming!" Clare paddled hard. She'd been frightened enough herself. She couldn't imagine how scary the flood must be for a tiny baby. When the boat thunked against the house, Clare pulled the paddle inside and reached out to hold the window frame.

"I can take you up to the bridge," Clare said. "It's dry there."

The baby started crying again, and the woman looked down at Clare. "Where are your parents?"

"My mother is in Houston and my father . . ." Clare swallowed hard. Between getting Nana to safety and freeing the boat, she'd almost managed to forget that she had no idea. "He should be back soon. I'm not sure where he is, though."

"Oh, honey," the woman said.

Clare shook her head. She wasn't going to cry. "Let's go. Can you hand her down to me? Then you can climb in."

The woman leaned farther out the window. Her hands trembled as she held the wailing baby over the water. Clare wrapped an arm around the tiny girl and tucked her in close to her chest. With her other hand, she held the window frame to steady the boat as the mother climbed down. Once she'd settled in and taken her little girl back, the baby quieted.

Clare started paddling toward the bridge. "What's her name?" she asked.

"Christina," the woman said, bouncing the baby quietly in her arms. "I'm Jennifer. And you are?"

"Clare."

"Thank you, Clare." Tears trailed down the

woman's cheeks. "I don't know what we would have done."

"You're safe now," Clare said. It made her feel good to help when the day had felt so out of control. "My neighbor says once you get to the bridge, you'll be able to walk to the Superdome. It's open as a shelter."

Jennifer nodded, and then the only sound was the paddle shushing through the dark water. Sweat dripped into Clare's eyes. She was working hard, and the sun had come out. It was hot.

Ranger settled down beside Jennifer and sniffed at the baby. She smelled like soap and milk that had spilled a long time ago.

A block from the bridge, Ranger heard more people sounds. He barked and pawed at Clare until she stopped paddling.

Then she heard it, too. A new voice calling out, "Help! I'm trapped up here!"

Clare paddled toward the sound until she spotted an older man waving a blue shirt out his window. "Help! Please!" he called.

The boat was already low in the water. But the man was skinny and frail. He didn't weigh enough to sink them, did he? It didn't matter. Clare knew she couldn't leave him behind.

She paddled the boat to the window and held it steady while he climbed on board.

"Praise the Lord," he said as Clare started paddling again. The boat was tippy now. They needed to get to the bridge.

But more voices called out. "Help us! Over here!"

Clare's heart sank when she saw four people on a roof halfway down a side street. There was no way they'd fit in the tiny flat-bottomed boat. Water was already sloshing over the side. Why couldn't it be bigger?

Clare raised her paddle into the air and

waved so they would know she saw them. "I'll send help!" she shouted. "I'll tell them you're here!"

When Clare got closer to the bridge, she realized she wasn't the only boat in the water at all. Other neighbors were delivering people to the bridge in their little fishing boats, too. They were dropping off passengers and turning right around to paddle back into the flood. Clare didn't see any of the Coast Guard vessels Mr. Robinson had promised, but her community was busy rescuing itself.

"Here we go . . . careful," Clare said as their little boat scraped onto the ramp of the bridge. She took the old man's hand while he climbed onto the bridge. She held little Christina while Jennifer stepped out of the boat.

Jennifer took her baby back and waited for Clare. "Aren't you coming?"

Clare looked up the ramp. Dozens of people

were walking toward the Superdome. No one seemed to notice her or the dog in the boat. They were all focused on getting to safety. Finding a dry place to sleep and probably water and something to eat other than soggy bread.

Then Clare looked back at the flooded streets of the Lower Ninth Ward. She thought of the people shouting from their rooftops. How many more neighbors were trapped in attics or watching out their windows, waiting for help? And what about her father? What if he'd made it back and found shelter with someone as the storm hit? What if he was trapped on a roof with the water rising, too?

Leave no one behind, Clare thought. She looked up at Jennifer and shook her head. "Be safe," she said.

And she paddled back into the flood.

Chapter 10

RUNAWAY HOUSE!

Ranger sat in the bow of the boat as Clare steered them away from the bridge. He shifted his weight from paw to paw. The air was wet and heavy with danger. He wished Clare would go with the mother and baby, where it was safe.

Ranger sniffed at Clare's garbage bag. His first aid kit was in there, all quiet. That meant his work wasn't finished. But Ranger was thirsty. He whined a little and pawed at Clare's arm.

"I know, dog," she said. "But we can't leave the boat and run off when people need help.

Our mission is to get those people off the roof." She gave Ranger a scratch behind his ear. Then she pulled her water bottle from her backpack and took a sip. She held Ranger's chin and dribbled water into his mouth, too.

"Ready?" Clare headed down the street.

Where had those people been? Clare paddled up to a pecan tree sticking out of the water. She wrapped an arm around it to keep the boat from drifting while she tried to figure out where she was. Everything looked different in the flood.

Suddenly, Ranger heard a creak and a groan. He sat tall in the boat and pricked up his ears.

"What was that?" Clare stared at a nearby house and realized that the flood had swept it off its foundation. It was all crooked, stuck between another house and a tree. "Hello?" Clare called out. "Is anyone there? Are you all right?"

The only answer was a loud, low scraping sound. The house groaned and shuddered. Then it scraped past the tree and came floating down the street toward them.

"Oh!" Clare let go of the tree. She plunged the paddle into the floodwater so hard and fast it got caught on a floating branch and twisted out of her hands.

"No!" Clare shouted. She lunged for the paddle. The tiny boat tipped dangerously to the side. But she was so close!

Clare leaned a little farther. Just as her fingertips brushed the paddle, the boat lurched. Clare fell on her back on the floor and looked up to see the drifting house looming over her.

Now they were trapped between the pecan tree and the house. The surging current was pushing it closer and closer. Their tiny boat would be in splinters in seconds. They'd drown if they weren't crushed first!

Clare hugged her garbage bag to her chest. "Jump!" she screamed, and leaped from the boat.

She clung to the plastic bundle and kicked as fast as she could. It felt as if each of her sneakers weighed a hundred pounds, but she forced herself to kick harder. She fought the urge to look back at the floating house threatening to crush her.

Clare gagged on mouthfuls of awful water as she swam. Was it even water anymore? No. It was a horrible, flooded-city soup that stank of sewage and chemicals and gasoline. Her arms cramped from holding so tightly to her bag. Her legs burned. Her eyes and nose stung. She wasn't sure how much longer she could swim. And then what?

Something crunched behind her. It sounded like a bundle of branches snapping in a giant's fist. Clare let herself stop swimming. Floating in the black water, she turned and saw the pieces that remained of her father's boat. The house had crushed it against the tree. If Clare had stayed in that boat, it would have been her limbs crunching against the tree. And the dog . . .

Where was he?

"Dog!" Clare called, and got a mouthful of awful water. She spit it out. "Dog!"

She heard a weak bark and whirled around. There he was! Closer to the house. It was wedged between two trees now and had stopped moving.

Clare kicked her way over to Ranger. With the boat shattered into toothpicks, the house was their only hope to get out of the water. Clare grabbed a window frame and flung her garbage bag onto the gently sloped roof. Then she grabbed the gutter and hoisted herself up.

The gutter creaked, but Clare held on. For

once, she was thankful Dad had forced her through his special "army training." She'd done push-ups and pull-ups in the yard with him three times a week since she was seven.

Now Clare used every bit of her strength. The sharp edge of the metal gutter cut into her palms, but she didn't let go. Finally, she collapsed on the roof. She caught her breath and turned to lean over the edge.

"Come on, dog, jump!" Clare called down to Ranger in the water below. She thumped the roof with her palm. "Up! Let's go!"

Ranger looked at Clare. How was he supposed to jump onto the roof when his legs were busy paddling?

He swam closer. The shingles were just inches above the water. But every time Ranger managed to get his paws onto the roof, they slid off again.

Clare leaned out as far as she dared. She

grabbed Ranger under his armpits and pulled him forward until he managed to get his front paws onto the roof. Then he caught his back paws on the gutter and scrambled the rest of the way up, knocking Clare over.

"Whoa!" Clare tumbled backward. She started to slide down the roof, but her sneakers caught on the gutter, and she carefully eased herself back up.

Ranger shook water from his fur. The house was shaky and creaky under his paws. A piece of siding ripped loose and floated down the street. Then another. And another.

Clare pressed her hands against the rough shingles, trembling. How long would it be before the whole soggy house broke into pieces and dumped them into the flood?

Chapter 11

HOPE FROM THE SKY

Clare looked up, searching the sky. A few rescue helicopters were buzzing around in the distance, but they were too far away to see her.

Clare wished she had a flag or bedsheet to wave. Something bigger and brighter than Nana's purple bandanna.

The house lurched. Clare braced herself to be thrown into the water, but it was only settling, still stuck between the trees. Clare hoped the trees were strong enough to hold it. She leaned over the gutter a bit to see if they were bending.

When she did, she saw a flash of bright orange. Dad's rain jacket from the boat! It was snagged on a jagged bit of wood floating by. Clare lay down on her belly. She stretched out her arm and tried not to think about the snakes wrapped around the life jacket earlier. When the edge of a sleeve brushed her hand, she closed her fingers around it and pulled it in.

"Yes!" Clare waved the bright jacket over her head. But when she looked up, even the distant helicopters had disappeared.

"Come back!" she shouted, though she knew no one could hear her.

Clare's eyes filled. But she took a deep breath and spread out Dad's orange jacket on the roof. She made it as big as she could.

Ranger flopped down on the jacket, but Clare shooed him off it. "We have to make sure the helicopter people see that. When they come back, they'll find us," she told Ranger. "They have to come back. There are still people left behind." She leaned into his damp fur and gave him a squeeze. "Dogs, too."

Ranger licked Clare's hand and tried to be a good listener. But he was thirsty. He was hungry. And the helicopters were all gone.

Clare tried to nap, but it was too hot. Yesterday's wind had threatened to blow the whole world apart, and today she couldn't even catch a breeze. She took out *Bud, Not Buddy*. It was all soggy, but she could still make out the words. She read a few chapters aloud to Ranger.

"Rules and things number eighty-three," Clare read. "If an adult tells you not to worry, and you weren't worried before, you better hurry up and start 'cause you're already running late."

Clare almost laughed. That wasn't really advice she needed. She'd been worrying for three days. She wished Nana were there to give her a hug and remind her not to fret.

Actually, no. She didn't want Nana anywhere near this awful, smelly water. Hopefully, Nana was safe at the Superdome with food and water and people taking care of her.

Clare wondered what time it was. The sun was finally setting, so it wasn't so hot. Would the helicopters come back? They couldn't just leave so many people behind, could they?

Clare slapped at a mosquito and wondered where her father was now. She'd tried not to think too much about why he hadn't come back. But she knew her father well enough to know that he would have come unless something had gone terribly wrong.

She leaned over and stroked Ranger's head. "We need to get off this roof, dog," she whispered. "Then we'll be able to find Nana and Dad. And everything will be okay."

They hadn't had anything to eat or drink all afternoon, so Clare untied the garbage bag, pulled out the water bottle, and held it between her knees. She unknotted the bag of bread, pulled out two pieces, and handed one to Ranger, who scarfed it up.

"I guess you were hungry, too," Clare said. She nibbled her own bread and shared the water with Ranger.

It was strange to see the city with all the electricity out. The sky was darker than she'd ever seen it. And it was so quiet. Usually, her neighborhood was full of the sounds of people talking and drinking sweet tea on their porches, playing music and laughing and grilling meat. But tonight, the only sound was the gurgle of floodwater.

Ranger crept onto Dad's jacket. This time, Clare let him stay. She curled up next to him, tried to ignore the mosquitoes whining in her ear, and closed her eyes.

Clare dreamed of helicopters that turned into giant insects and ropes that twisted into snakes.

She woke to Ranger licking her cheek and barking.

"What?" Clare blinked and leaned up on her elbows. The sky was a hazy pink color. It was getting warm again. She was out of water, and she couldn't imagine spending another day on this roof. Why couldn't the dog have let her sleep a little longer?

But Ranger kept barking. When he stopped for just a moment, Clare heard another sound.

The buzz of a helicopter. It was coming in from the river, headed right for her.

"Oh! Here!" she shouted, even though no one in the chopper could have heard her.

Clare grabbed her father's jacket, stood up, and waved it in a long arc over her head. "Over here!"

Clare squinted up at the big brown helicopter against the blue morning sky and said a silent prayer.

Please, God. Let them see.

Chapter 12

HELICOPTER RESCUE

Soon, the helicopter was overhead. Wind from its spinning rotor blasted hot air onto the roof. Clare stared up into the whirling blades.

"They see us!" she shouted to Ranger.

A side door opened, and a man in an orange suit appeared. He waved down at her, and Clare waved back. He turned away for a moment, and the next thing Clare knew, he was dangling in a harness on a cable, dropping down from the helicopter toward the roof. He wore a dark blue helmet, black gloves on his hands, and black boots. There were swimming fins hanging from his waist. Clare hoped that didn't mean they were going back in the water. Almost anywhere sounded better than this roof, though.

Clare pulled Ranger close. She grabbed her father's jacket, stuffed it into her garbage bag, and tied the bag closed just as the man's boots touched down on the roof.

"Hi, I'm Sara," the person said.

"Oh!" Clare stared. The man dangling from the cable wasn't a man at all. "You're a girl!"

"Yep. I'm also your rescue swimmer." Sara unclipped the cable from her harness and waved up at the helicopter. "Let's get you out of here, okay?"

"Yes, please," Clare said. She watched the cable swing as someone pulled it back into the helicopter. She looked at Sara's swim fins and then out at the mucky water. "Do we have to swim?"

"Nope," Sara said, and pointed up toward the helicopter. Now they were lowering some sort of giant metal laundry basket down on the cable. "You're getting a lift."

When the basket got close enough, Sara reached out and pulled it in until it was resting on the roof between Clare and Ranger. "Now," Sara said. "I need you to climb into the basket, sit down, and stay put. Keep your arms and legs inside so you're safe when you get up to the helicopter. And once you get up there, follow the directions of the person inside. Okay?"

"Okay." Clare started to climb into the basket with her bag. Then she looked back at Ranger. She couldn't leave him behind.

Sara seemed to read her mind. "Don't worry," she said. "There's room for your dog." She held Clare's hand to balance her as she settled in the basket. Then she lifted Ranger by his middle and plopped him in beside her.

"Ready?" Sara asked.

"Aren't you coming?" Clare said. She hadn't imagined dangling in the air all by herself.

"I'll go up on my harness after you're safe," Sara said. "All set?"

Clare's heart thudded in her chest, but she nodded. She wrapped one arm around her garbage bag and the other around Ranger. Sara held the guide wire with one hand. She waved at the helicopter. Then the steel cable lifted Clare and Ranger from the roof.

"Remember, hands inside!" Sara shouted as the basket began to spin. "I'll see you up there!"

Clare's stomach lurched as the basket twirled. She squeezed her eyes closed and felt the dog's warm body lean against her. Finally, she opened her eyes and looked out over her neighborhood.

Clare gasped. It was as if Lake Pontchartrain had swallowed up all of New Orleans. The black water was everywhere. Only the tops of trees and rooftops stuck out. Off in the distance, on the other side of the bridge, she could see some dry streets. Was that where Mr. Robinson had taken Nana?

The roar of the helicopter got louder and louder until Clare was right beneath it.

"Stay right there!" a man called from the open door. When the basket was level with the door, he reached out to pull Clare and Ranger inside. Their basket slid onto the helicopter floor.

"You all right?" the man asked as he took Clare's hand.

Clare nodded and let him help her climb out.

"Have a seat on the floor over there," he said. "We're going to take you to the highway.

Buses will be waiting there to take everyone to the shelter."

Ranger climbed out of the basket, too. The helicopter was packed with people and full of strong smells — gasoline and floodwater and wet wool blankets.

Clare pulled Ranger over to a spot away from the door, next to an older lady who reminded her of Nana. She watched the helicopter door until Sara climbed back inside. Then the door closed, and they started moving.

Where? Clare wasn't sure. She couldn't stop thinking about all the flooded neighborhoods. The crowds of people walking through rivers of muck on the streets. Where were they all going? And how would she ever find her family among them?

Chapter 13

TURNED AWAY

The helicopter soared over the flooded streets and finally hovered above a crowded highway overpass. Police cleared people away so it could land. Clare climbed out onto the steaming asphalt with her garbage bag over her shoulder. "Here, dog!" she called, and waited for Ranger to jump down beside her.

"Good boy." Clare gave Ranger a scratch behind his ear. Then she looked around for the buses that were supposed to take them to the Superdome six miles away.

All she saw were police cars, a lonely Red

Cross van, and a long line of people waiting for water. Clare brought Ranger to the end of the line.

"Do you know when the buses are coming?" she asked when she got to the front.

"Maybe this afternoon," a woman said, and handed Clare a bottle of water.

"Thank you." Clare tried not to guzzle it too fast. She bent down and dribbled some water into Ranger's mouth, then took another drink. Even warm, the water was amazing. She hadn't realized how much her throat hurt.

"Don't worry," the Red Cross woman said. "You'll be safe in Baton Rouge before you know it."

"Baton Rouge!" Clare nearly choked on the water. Baton Rouge was an hour-and-a-half drive on a good day. "I thought the buses were taking us to the Superdome!"

"Oh, no," the woman said. "We're evacuating the city at this point." She turned to help someone else.

Clare's thoughts swirled like leaves in the storm. She couldn't go to Baton Rouge. She had to find Nana at the Superdome!

Clare looked around and tried to get her bearings. She'd been to the big stadium once for a football game with her dad and Uncle Jay. Could she find her way? She felt like a ghost walking through the crowd. No one seemed to notice her at all.

With Ranger at her side, Clare walked down the highway until she found an exit ramp. The streets weren't as flooded here, but the whole city felt dirty and wet. People wandered with stuffed pillowcases and garbage bags like Clare's. Some dragged suitcases. Everyone wore the same tired expression.

At least Clare didn't need to worry about

finding the Superdome. Everyone was going there. She and Ranger shuffled along with the crowd for more than two hours. Finally, she could see the Superdome's battered roof. The storm had ripped off huge pieces and thrown them into the street.

As Clare and Ranger approached, guards blocked the road.

Some people started shouting. Clare walked carefully up to a police officer. "Please," she said. "Can you help me? I have to get to the Superdome."

"It's way over capacity," he said. "And trust me. It's not a place you want to be right now anyway. There's not enough food or water, and tempers are running hot. You'll have to go to the convention center."

"But my grandmother's here!" Clare cried. "She's sick. I have to find her."

"If she's sick, she's already been evacuated."

The officer looked down at Clare. He lowered his voice. "Your best bet is actually in Gretna. I heard there are buses there now. Food and water, too. And once you get to Baton Rouge, you'll be able to find your grandmother."

"Gretna?" Clare said.

"That's right." The officer pointed in the direction of the Mississippi River. "Over the bridge." Then he turned away.

Clare was so tired and hungry she couldn't think straight. She needed to find Nana and her father. Were they in Gretna? Who could tell? But food and water and buses seemed like a good start. They'd already walked six miles. What was another two?

Clare led Ranger down the street toward the Crescent City Connection, the big bridge over the Mississippi River. Lots of other people were going the same way. With every block, the crowd got bigger.

Finally, Clare led Ranger onto the bridge on-ramp, and they melted into the crowd. Clare found herself walking beside two ladies pulling suitcases. She figured they must be from out of town. They sure had picked an awful time to visit New Orleans.

"Are you all right?" one of the women asked Clare. "Here." The woman pulled a bottle of water and a couple of granola bars from her bag and handed them to Clare. "The hotel where we were staying had to evacuate, but they sent us off with water and snacks."

The ladies waited while Clare had some water and gave Ranger a little, too. "Thank you," Clare said as they started walking onto the bridge.

Clare was daydreaming about cold water and real food and a hug from her dad when, suddenly, the crowd stopped moving. Had they reached the buses already?

Clare's heart sped up. "Come on, dog," she

said. "Let's see what's happening!" She weaved through the crowd to the front.

There were no buses. They'd stopped because a line of policemen stretched across the bridge. The officers were holding guns and shouting. When a few of the men in the crowd tried to go talk with them, an officer fired his gun into the air.

Ranger whined. The gunshot hurt his ears. Something about these men felt desperate. Dangerous. He pawed at Clare until she backed away.

Clare waited in the crowd with a sinking feeling in her chest. They couldn't have come all this way only to be turned back. Why? Why would anyone stop people who needed help from getting it? It had to be a mistake.

But the angry voices got louder.

"Back away! Get off this bridge!" one of the officers shouted.

"We're not going to have another Superdome here!" another voice boomed.

More gunshots rang out, and Clare found herself swept up in a river of people retreating. Away from the bridge. Away from safety and water and food. Her eyes filled with hot tears.

If Dad were here, he would have talked his way over that bridge. He'd have them all on a bus with water. She needed her father. He had to be back in the city by now, didn't he?

Clare imagined herself walking the streets and calling his name. "Dad! Lamont Porter! Dad!" She tried to imagine him answering, running down the street to wrap her up in his big arms and tell her everything would be all right. But no matter how hard she tried, she couldn't see that happening.

Chapter 14

THIS LITTLE LIGHT

"Come on, dog," Clare struggled to keep her voice from trembling. "We're going to the convention center."

She hadn't decided until she said it. But if her father was in the city, he'd look there eventually, wouldn't he? And if he wasn't ... well ... Clare tried not to think about that.

When they were almost to the convention center, a stray dog stepped out of a doorway, growling. Clare backed away, but the dog crept closer.

The hair on Ranger's neck prickled. This

German shepherd reminded him of the unfriendly dogs at the park. Usually, it was best to stay away from those dogs, but it was too late for that. The dog stepped forward and snapped at Clare's ankle.

Ranger growled low in his throat. He lunged at the other dog, barking his biggest bark.

The dog ran off down the street. Ranger didn't stop barking until it turned the corner.

Clare sank to her knees and hugged him. "Thank you, dog." She wiped a tear from her cheek with Nana's old bandanna and then stared down at it. Where was Nana? Had someone already taken her on a bus to Baton Rouge? Or was she here somewhere, hurting?

The dog had managed to find Nana once before after he'd sniffed at the jacket she left behind. Clare held out the bandanna. "Can you smell Nana?"

Ranger sniffed the damp, purple cloth. He

smelled Clare's tears and floodwater and helicopter fumes. But there was another scent, too. The old woman he'd found before. The one he'd waited with in the steamy attic before the boat took her away. Ranger looked up at Clare.

"Can you smell her?" Clare asked. "If she's here, we need to find her!"

Find! Ranger thought back to his training with Luke and Dad. Sometimes, when the air was just right and there wasn't too much wind, it was easy to find the person he was supposed to find. But when it was raining too hard or when there were lots of other smells, it was more difficult. Ranger knew today would be one of those times.

Clare pulled open the door of the convention center. A wave of heat and sour smells rushed out. It was dark inside, even in the middle of the day. But if Nana was in there, she needed help.

Clare said, "Come on, dog! Let's find Nana," and they stepped inside.

When Clare's eyes adjusted to the darkness, her heart sank. Little kids were running around crying. Was anyone taking care of them? Old men and women leaned against every wall, their eyes closed. It looked as if no one had enough food or water. Everyone was waiting. For what? Buses that might never arrive?

Clare held out the bandanna to Ranger. "Come on . . . let's find her. Find Nana?"

Ranger breathed in the Nana smell and set off through the crowd. There were so many people. Too many smells! Finally, he turned a hallway corner.

There!

Ranger followed the Nana scent down the hallway into a room that was even more crowded. People were sprawled on the floor. Many were old and sick. Some had gone to the bathroom in their clothes, and no one was cleaning them up.

Clare lifted the bandanna to her mouth and breathed through it. Was Nana in this awful place?

Ranger stepped through the mob, toward a row of people sitting up in chairs by the wall. The Nana smell was getting stronger.

There! Ranger barked.

"Nana!" Clare called out and ran to her. Nana was slumped over in a folding chair, but when Clare shouted, her eyes fluttered open.

"Oh, Nana!" Clare sank to her knees and buried her head in her grandmother's lap.

Nana lifted a hand and stroked Clare's hair. "Praise the Lord," she said. Her voice was dry

and gravelly. She coughed and couldn't stop for a long time. When she did, her eyes were red and watery. "Your father will be right back," she said.

"Oh, Nana." Clare's eyes filled with tears. Nana was so confused she still thought Dad was coming back with the car. "He got stuck somewhere when he went out to put gas in the car. We have to get out of here, to safety. The buses . . ."

Clare sighed. She didn't believe in buses anymore. They might as well have been waiting for fairies or unicorns to rescue them. She'd found Nana, and what could she do for her? Nothing except wait and hope.

Clare took a deep, shaky breath. "There are buses coming," she said. "Eventually. They'll take us to safety."

Clare tried to sound confident. But she

knew Nana was struggling. What if the buses arrived too late?

Clare had been so strong. Now she slumped against the wall beside Nana's chair. After a few minutes, she felt a hand on her shoulder.

Nana started singing the song she'd sung when Clare was little. "This little light of mine . . . I'm gonna let it shine . . ."

Tears filled Clare's eyes. But her heart filled with hope. Even with Nana's raspy, dry throat, she was singing. It made Clare feel like she might be able to sing, too.

"This little light of mine . . ." Clare sang. "I'm gonna let it shine. This little light of mine . . . I'm gonna let it shine . . ."

A woman shuffling by with a baby in her arms stopped. "Let it shine," she sang with them. Another woman joined in. "Let it shine, let it shine."

Clare felt her frustration and fear and rage lift away with every note. But when the song ended, she and Nana were alone again.

"Your father will be back any minute," Nana said.

"Thanks, Nana." Clare couldn't bear to tell her the truth. Dad wasn't here. And she didn't even know if he was alive.

Chapter 15

No Dogs Allowed

Soon, Nana was snoring quietly. Clare hugged her dad's orange jacket to her chest. Somehow, it still smelled like her father on a boating day — like sweat and shaving lotion and blue crabs. "Where are you?" Clare whispered into the dark. "Why can't you find us?"

Find? Ranger sat up.

"What is it, dog?" She looked down at the jacket. "This is Dad's," she said. "But he's not here."

Ranger pawed at the jacket. Clare held it

out, and he sniffed it. It smelled like Clare and floodwater and fish, but there was another smell, too. A person smell.

Ranger barked and stood up. Clare looked down at Nana's purple bandanna. The dog had used it to find her. Could he find Clare's father, too?

Clare looked at Ranger and felt an impossible hope. She tied the bandanna around his neck and gave him a quick hug. "Go on then, dog," she whispered. "I have to stay with Nana, but go. Find Dad if you can."

Ranger sniffed the jacket again and walked into the crowd. There were so many smells here. Spoiling food and sickness and sweat. He waited until someone opened a door and slipped outside. He walked up and down both sides of the street. When he was almost back to Clare and Nana, he hesitated.

There! It was faint, but it was there. Ranger

tracked the Dad smell to the end of the block, up to a big truck where two men were handing out water. He ran up to the taller man and barked.

"Whose dog?" the man said, looking around. He shook his head and went back to work.

Ranger pawed at the man's leg. The man looked down, scowling. But then he reached out and touched the purple bandanna around the dog's neck. His face changed. He turned to the other man and said, "I'll be right back."

Ranger led the man into the building. He pushed through the crowd until he saw Clare and Nana. Then he barked.

Clare looked up. "Daddy!" She raced into his arms.

"Praise the Lord," he whispered into her hair. He held her back to look at her, then knelt beside Nana. "You found her!"

"She found me," Nana said. "I told her you were here, but she didn't believe me."

Her father laughed a little. Then his eyes filled with tears. He turned to Clare. "There was no gasoline anywhere. I had to leave the city to fill the tank. And then . . ." He blinked hard. "Then they were turning people around. I tried every back road you can imagine. When the storm swept in, a tree fell in the middle of the road and I got stranded."

"How did you get back?" Clare asked.

"Walked," he said. "Thirty miles, best as I can tell. I found Nana yesterday and hooked up with guys from my army unit to help out with supplies. It's been a mess, but buses will be here in the morning. Now that we found you, we can leave for Houston." He motioned for Clare to sit down. Then he settled next to her and pulled her in close. "Try to get some rest," he said. "And hey . . . where'd the dog come from?"

"I'm not sure," Clare patted Ranger on the head. "We adopted him. Or maybe he adopted us."

Her father looked at Ranger and ran a hand over his collar. "He looks pretty well cared for, Clare. Probably just got separated from his owner in the storm. Hope he finds his way home."

Ranger curled up next to Clare, beside the garbage bag. His first aid kit was in there, still quiet. Hadn't he done his job? He'd kept Clare safe. He'd found Nana and Dad. When would he get to go home?

In the morning, a long line of buses stretched down the street. A man in a uniform motioned

Clare's family into line. But when they got to the bus, he held up his hand.

"No dogs," he said.

"I can't leave him behind," Clare said. Not now. She couldn't.

The man knelt and put a hand on Clare's shoulder. "I'm afraid you'll have to. But there are groups working to gather pets left behind. He'll be cared for. They should be able to return him to you when you come home."

Clare looked at the shaggy golden dog. She put down her garbage bag, knelt, and hugged him. He had a home somewhere. She knew that. But she was so glad he'd been hers for a little while. She tugged gently at Nana's purple bandanna around his neck. "You can keep this, okay? It looks good on you. And it'll help you remember us." Clare gave him one last squeeze and started to tie her garbage bag shut again.

Ranger pawed at the bag. There was a quiet humming sound inside. It was already getting louder.

"What do you want, dog?" Clare opened the bag, and Ranger's first aid kit fell out onto the sidewalk.

"Oh!" Clare said. "That's yours! Here . . ." She put the leather strap around Ranger's neck. She couldn't hear the humming, but Ranger already felt heat growing at his throat.

"Clare, let's go, baby!" her father called from the bus.

"Good-bye, dog!" Clare gave him one last squeeze, and whispered, "I hope you find your way home, too." Then she ran to the bus. Her father had already helped Nana into a seat. Clare sat across from them by a window.

Ranger watched more people file onto the bus. The first aid kit was humming loudly now. Light was beginning to spill from the cracks, but he kept his eyes on Clare's face in the window until the bus finally pulled away. The humming had grown so loud that it drowned out the bus motors and people talking. The light grew brighter and brighter. Finally, Ranger had to close his eyes. He felt as if he were being squeezed through a hole in the sky.

When the humming stopped, Ranger opened his eyes and saw rain pouring down.

Chapter 16

GOING HOME

The sky rumbled. But it was home thunder. And Ranger was standing next to his dog bed, right there in the mudroom where he'd left it. Ranger walked over and lowered his head so the first aid kit dropped onto his bed.

"Don't worry, Ranger," Luke said as he walked in with the ketchup and mustard bottles. "It's not a very big storm. Should pass by soon, and then we can go back outside." He looked down at Ranger and tipped his head. "Where'd you get the bandanna? Have Sadie and Noreen been dressing you up again?"

Ranger pawed at the bandanna. Luke knelt down and untied it. Ranger took it gently in his teeth and dropped it in his bed. "That's fair," Luke said, laughing. "If they want to tie some weird purple scarf around your neck, I guess you can do whatever you want with it."

Luke headed into the kitchen. "Come on, Ranger! Dad made peanut butter cookies!"

Ranger barked, but he didn't follow Luke right away. Instead, he pawed at his blanket until the first aid kit and the faded purple bandanna were covered up. He'd miss Clare's neck scratches and her singing. But somehow he knew that Clare was safe now, too.

Outside the thunder rumbled again, but it didn't seem so bad. Ranger was glad his work was finally done. Just like Clare, he was safe with his family now. And there were cookies waiting in the kitchen.

AUTHOR'S NOTE

Clare Porter is a fictional character, but her story is based on the experiences of real-life people who survived Hurricane Katrina in the Lower Ninth Ward in New Orleans in 2005. Katrina was one of the deadliest hurricanes in American history. When the storm surge arrived in New Orleans on the morning of August 29, the flood protection system failed in dozens of places, leaving 80 percent of the city underwater. At least 1,836 people died, and more than a million more had to leave their homes, including around 160,000 children like Clare.

Even though New Orleans was under a

mandatory evacuation order, many people couldn't leave before the storm hit. Some didn't have cars. Some had elderly or sick relatives who couldn't be moved. Some didn't have enough money to leave town. New Orleans's poorest residents were hit the hardest. The sequence of events Clare experiences in this story is based on real people's recollections, shared in books, museums, online, and in personal interviews.

Rising floodwaters forced many people, like Clare, to break out of their attics and wait on rooftops for help. Some Lower Ninth Ward residents took their small boats out to rescue neighbors. The woman in the helicopter who rescues Clare and Ranger from the roof was inspired by Sara Faulkner, a real Coast Guard rescue swimmer who was working in New Orleans in the days that followed Hurricane Katrina.

Sara, who was the first woman to graduate from the Coast Guard's rigorous training program and then serve as a rescue swimmer, was kind enough to talk with me about her work that week and walk me through what Clare would have experienced when the helicopter arrived.

Clare's story of being turned away on the bridge, sadly, is also based on a real event. On September 1, 2005, hundreds of people who had been forced out of their homes and hotels were trying to walk over the Crescent City Connection to the nearby city of Gretna. Police officers blocked pedestrians from crossing the bridge. Gretna was closed, they said. Officers ordered the flood survivors back to New Orleans and fired shotguns over their heads. New Orleans residents were angry that even elderly people and children were turned away, and there were accusations of racism. Most of the officers were white, and most of the people in the crowd were black. One of the officers reportedly told the crowd, "We're not going to have any Superdomes over here." Gretna's police chief defended his decision to close the bridge. He said no one warned him people would be coming from New Orleans, so his city was overwhelmed and not prepared to handle the large crowds trying to escape the flooded city.

Many residents of the Lower Ninth Ward remain angry about how they were treated in the days that followed Hurricane Katrina. They'll never forget how long it took the federal government to send buses and aid. A photograph of President George W. Bush viewing the flooded city from the safety of a helicopter high above hangs at the Lower Ninth Ward Living Museum — a reminder of how forgotten people in the Lower Ninth

Ward felt as they waited for help to arrive. But this tiny museum in a formerly flooded home also tells the story of a community that came together — neighbors rescuing neighbors, heading back into the flood to do the work they feared no one else would.

Another New Orleans museum, the Presbytère, has a Hurricane Katrina exhibit with personal accounts and artifacts from those late summer days in 2005. Among them is an artifact from one of Katrina's most famous survivors, musician Fats Domino, who was rescued from his Lower Ninth Ward home. His piano didn't survive the flood; what's left of it is on display in the museum's lobby.

Before Hurricane Katrina, Clare's Lower Ninth Ward neighborhood was known as a place where neighbors gathered on their porches to visit over sweet tea and music after supper. It's a community full of pride and history — the first area of the Deep South to desegregate its schools during the Civil Rights movement. Ruby Bridges, an African-American girl who had to be escorted to school by federal marshals to protect her from angry white residents, attended William Frantz Elementary in the Ninth

Ward. This was also the first area of the city where African-American people who had once been enslaved were able to own property. Before Katrina, the Ninth Ward had one of the highest rates of home ownership in the city. Houses had been passed down from generation to generation, and more than half of the fifteen thousand people who lived there owned their homes outright.

When I visited the Lower Ninth Ward in December of 2016, the population had only recovered to around 2,800 people. Eleven years after Katrina, just two of the neighborhood's seven public schools had reopened. Many homes are still in ruins. One hundred percent of the houses in the Lower Ninth were uninhabitable after the storm. Some were completely washed away. Those that weren't were full of toxic black mold because water was left standing so long after the storm.

The scars from Katrina still run deep as you drive through the streets of this neighborhood. Many houses were never rebuilt. It's not uncommon to see porch steps leading to nowhere.

Some buildings still have what's known as the Katrina cross spray-painted on the siding. It was a system rescue workers used to show which homes had been searched, how many people had been found alive, and how many hadn't survived.

Ranger's experience being left behind when the buses pulled out of the city was one that happened to tens of thousands of New Orleans pets. While some rescuers allowed people to bring pets along in boats and helicopters, there was no official policy on rescuing animals, so many also refused.

An estimated 250,000 pets were left behind when their owners evacuated due to Hurricane Katrina. While animal rescue groups worked heroically to help stranded pets and reunite them with their owners, more than half of the pets stranded by Katrina died or were never found.

This led to some changes in both state and federal laws. In 2006, Congress passed the Pets Evacuation and Transportation Standards Act, or PETS Act, which authorized federal rescuers to rescue pets along with people in natural disasters. After

Hurricane Katrina, officials realized that many people who refuse to evacuate in advance of a storm make that decision because they don't want to leave their pets behind. Because of this, they expect that the PETS Act will save not only animals' lives but people's lives as well.

While there have been some positive outcomes after Hurricane Katrina, residents of the Lower Ninth Ward still feel ignored. Some say that construction debris left in the streets, broken fire hydrants, and uncovered storm drains make them feel like the city of New Orleans has given up on them.

But for many, the Lower Ninth Ward will always be home. An organization called lowernine.org has been working since the storm to help the residents return and reclaim their property. Since 2005, the group's workers and volunteers have rebuilt eighty-four houses and completed 250 more renovation projects.

The damage from Hurricane Katrina was devastating. But every year, volunteers make

a little more progress as they work with members of the community to bring a neighborhood back to life. If your family or class would like to help with that work, you can make a donation at http://lowernine.org.

FURTHER READING

If you'd like to read more stories about Hurricane Katrina and real-life search-and-rescue dogs, check out the following books and websites:

"Eye on the Storm: Hurricane Katrina Fast Facts" by Brian Handwerk, via National Geographic: http://news.nationalgeographic.com/news/2005/09/0906_050906_katrina_facts.html

Marvelous Cornelius: Hurricane Katrina and the Spirit of New Orleans by Phil Bildner, illustrated by John Parra (Chronicle Books, 2015)

A Place Where Hurricanes Happen by Renee Watson, illustrated by Shadra Strickland (Random House, 2010)

Sniffer Dogs: How Dogs (and Their Noses) Save

the World by Nancy Castaldo (Houghton Mifflin Harcourt, 2014)

Two Bobbies: A True Story of Hurricane Katrina, Friendship, and Survival by Kirby Larson and Mary Nethery, illustrated by Jean Cassels (Bloomsbury, 2008)

What was Hurricane Katrina? by Robin Koontz, illustrated by John Hinderliter (Grosset & Dunlap, 2015)

SOURCES

I'm grateful to Laura Paul from lowernine .org for sharing her group's story and showing me around the neighborhood, and to J. F. "Smitty" Smith for sharing his reflections of living through Hurricane Katrina and its aftermath. Mr. Smith wrote his own book about the disaster, called *Exiled in Paradise*. He was especially helpful in talking with me about the frustration and sense of betrayal that people in the Lower Ninth still feel, more than a decade after the storm. "This was a tough blow for all of us," he said. "You spend forty-five years getting your house together, and all of a sudden it's gone. And the state, local, and federal government doesn't want to help you out." Both Paul and Smith read early drafts of this manuscript, and I'm so thankful for their helpful feedback.

Dave Lewald, who was in command of the waterborne contingent of the US Coast Guard's response in New Orleans, provided helpful information about the days that followed the storm, and Coast Guard rescue swimmer Sara Faulkner shared her amazing Katrina rescue stories with me as well. Thanks, too, to the curators at the Lower Ninth Ward Living Museum and Presbytère for answering my many questions. The following sources were also helpful in my research:

American Rescue Dog Association. *Search and Rescue Dogs: Training the K-9 Hero.* 2nd ed. New York: Wiley Publishing, 2002.

Brinkley, Douglas. *The Great Deluge: Hurricane Katrina, New Orleans, and the Mississippi Gulf Coast.* New York: William Morrow, 2006.

Fothergill, Alice, and Lori Peek. *Children of Katrina*. Austin, TX: University of Texas Press, 2015.

Horne, Jed. *Breach of Faith: Hurricane Katrina and the Near Death of a Great American City*. New York: Random House, 2006.

Levitt, Jeremy L., and Matthew C. Whitaker, eds. *Hurricane Katrina: America's Unnatural Disaster*. Lincoln, NE: University of Nebraska Press, 2009.

60 Minutes. "The Bridge to Gretna." December 15, 2005. http://www.cbsnews.com/news/the-bridge-to-gretna/

Wilkinson, Lynette Norris. *Untold: The New Orleans 9th Ward You Never Knew*. New Orleans: Write Creations, 2010.

ABOUT THE AUTHOR

Kate Messner is the author of *The Seventh Wish*; *All the Answers*; *The Brilliant Fall of Gianna Z.*, recipient of the E. B. White Read Aloud Award for Older Readers; *Capture the Flag*, a Crystal Kite Award winner; *Over and Under the Snow*, a *New York Times* Notable Children's Book; and the Ranger in Time and Marty McGuire chapter book series. A former middle-school English teacher, Kate lives on Lake Champlain with her family and loves reading, walking in the woods, and traveling. Visit her online at www.katemessner.com.

Everyone says the *Titanic* is unsinkable, and Patrick Murphy believes this most of all. He works at the shipyard where the *Titanic* was built, and he's even going on its maiden voyage! Ranger meets Patrick before the *Titanic* sets sail. One night, the ship hits an iceberg and starts to take on water, and then it's a race against time to evacuate passengers before it's too late.

Keep reading for a sneak peek!

Patrick and Ranger hurried up to the deck. Everyone was talking at once.

"Is everything all right?"

"Why have we stopped?"

"It's fine," one of the crewmen told a group of passengers. "You can go back to bed."

Some people returned to their cabins. Others huddled in their nightgowns on the deck.

"It was an iceberg, I tell you," someone said. "Saw the huge white mass myself when I looked out my porthole. Like a mountain on the sea."

"Come on, dog," Patrick said, hurrying toward the bow of the ship. Ranger followed Patrick, but the fur on his neck prickled. The air smelled icy and fishy and dangerous. Then Ranger felt something cold under his paw. He barked and stepped back.

Patrick bent down, picked up a chunk of ice, and sucked in his breath. "We must have hit ice," he whispered. He looked out into the darkness and tried to stay calm. *This ship was designed to sail through icy waters*, he reminded himself.

Sure enough, the engines chugged to life, and the ship started moving.

Patrick let out a whoosh of breath. "See, dog?" he said. "Everything is fine."

Then the engines stopped again.

Two firemen came rushing up the steps. "She's flooding!" one of them shouted.

"Go wake the first-class passengers," an officer told Patrick. "Get them up to the boat deck in their life jackets. Tell them it's just a precaution. We don't want to alarm them."

Patrick hesitated. "Is there cause for alarm?"

The officer only pointed down the stairs. "Follow the order you've been given."

Patrick and Ranger hurried downstairs. They rushed up and down the first-class hallways. Ranger barked. Patrick pounded on cabin doors to wake people up. He helped them into their life jackets and sent them up to the deck.

"Is the ship actually taking on water?" one man asked Patrick. "Have you seen it for yourself?" He looked around his warm, dry cabin.

"No, sir," Patrick said. "But I've been told that everyone must head up to the boat deck now."

The man sighed. He pulled a coat on over his nightclothes and followed Patrick and Ranger down the hall and up the stairs.

When Patrick finished waking the first-class passengers in the hallway he'd been assigned, he ran downstairs to see the damage for himself. It would be on the lower levels of the ship, near the mail room and one of the boiler rooms. Ranger followed him, but with every flight of stairs they descended, the air smelled more dangerous. Like wet metal and seawater and ice.

MEET RANGER

A time–traveling golden retriever with search-and-rescue training . . . and a nose for danger!